Better Be FN Swole

Robert Frank

615 Publishing

Copyright © 2024 by Robert Frank.

Better be FN Swole, by Robert Frank.

All rights reserved. No part of this publication may be reproduced, distributed, or transmitted in any form or by any means, including photocopying, recording or other electronic or mechanical methods, without the prior written permission of the publisher, except in the case of brief quotations embodied in critical reviews and certain other, non-commercial uses permitted by copyright law.

First Edition, First Printing.

ISBN: 979-8-875-97479-3

Printed in the United States of America
1 2 3 4 5 6 7 8 9 10 29 28 27 26 25 24

Introduction

Robert here. Yes, it's really me writing this so if there happens to be any grammatical errors, we will blame the "Robert Frank" character for any mistakes. This is my first book going out to the world and I wanted to personally thank you for picking up Better Be FN Swole! The quotes you will read in this book come from the videos that have given the @Robertfrank615 social media pages a fresh coat of paint. These videos show a different side of the bandana wearing, angry meathead guy that screams in his car. It's still the same guy, just outside of the driver's seat, fully clothed, and actually.... having fun!

I will assume most of you reading this book know who I am. You're familiar with my content and you're shocked that I even have the capability to write a book. Some of you may not be that familiar with me, but you picked up the book because of the badass cover designed by the legendary Paul Huh. So let me give you the footnotes version of how these quotes came into existence.

I've been making videos for social media since 2012, but I am best known for my Car Rage videos from 2016-2020. Between all platforms combined, those videos have over 1 billion total views.

They've been shared by the biggest pages on the internet such as Worldstar, 9Gag, Unilad, Snoop Dogg, Barstool, Joe Rogan, and the list goes on. The jacked up, sweaty, shirtless meathead became a household face in the online fitness community. Even if people didn't know my name, they knew I was "that guy" who screams in his car.

Fast forward to 2021- when I spent most of the year in the hospital. I went from 212lbs to 138lbs in five weeks. Two emergency surgeries in a seven-day span, and five surgeries total thanks to Ulcerative Colitis.

I had my entire colon removed and had a colostomy bag on my stomach for 11 months. I was not the same "jacked and tan" guy that I once was. I lost all my GAINZ. To stay relevant and pump out content for my full-time job, social media, I needed to reinvent myself and the "Better Be FN Swole" videos were born.

As the popularity of TikTok was rising and attention spans were being destroyed across social media- long form content was becoming extinct. These videos came at the perfect time. They're all roughly 11-20 seconds long depending on the quote, perfect timing to hold the attention of anyone scrolling past on social media. I am also fully clothed in these videos, which also came at a perfect time because I am not the same aesthetic specimen that I once was. My physique is currently "under construction".

I will introduce you to my crew in the outro, but there have only been a handful of people who recorded these videos for me. As simple as it seems to pan up from my sneakers to my face, it's a special touch that first Joey Bags, and now Alex "The Latin Heartthrob" have. The secret sauce to these videos is whoever is holding the camera has NO IDEA what I am about to say. The reactions are genuine as they're hearing it for the first time. So, I know if they're laughing- you're laughing.

This is the longest introduction in the history of introductions, so let's get to the good shit. The quotes you are about to read are all thought of by ME. I don't use AI to make them, and I rarely take suggestions. You will notice that there are only "Chest Days" and "Arm Days" because in reality, what else is there? Feel free to replace Shoulders or Back in there if your little heart desires. Lastly, if there is a little story or translation to each quote, I will add it below. If there is no story, that means it's just some weird shit I thought of while driving or in the shower.

Enjoy the shit show…

"On Monday we do chest, cuz if you want to spray your ball sauce on her placenta, in the back of a Toyota Venza- your pecs better be FN swole!"

"On Tuesday we do arms, cuz if you want the waitress at Olive Garden tuggin on your weenie, before you bust a nut in the linguine- your arms better be FN swole!"

Fun fact- This video was the first one to be taken down by TikTok for a "community guidelines" violation. I don't see anything wrong AT ALL with this quote…

"On Wednesday we do arms, cuz if you want two thick chicks munching on your dingleberries, before you turn them over and bust on their bellies- your arms better be FN swole!"

"On Thursday we do arms, cuz if you want to take a thick chick out for sushi, before you cream pie her coochie- your arms better be FN swole!"

"On Friday we do arms, cuz if you want to slam your beef gavel all up in her queef chapel- your arms better be FN swole!"

"On Saturday we do arms, cuz if you want your mushroom tip blasting goo on her lips, in a Mitsubishi Eclipse- your arms better be FN swole!"

"On Sunday we do arms, cuz if you want to go to the nursing home and get some granny cooter, beat her in checkers than take off on her scooter- your arms better be FN swole!"

"On Monday we do chest, cuz if you want a thick mami screaming mas chorizo duro por favor, in the back of a Rav 4- your pecs better be FN swole!"

Fun fact- English translation is "give me hard sausage please".

"On Taco Tuesday we do arms, cuz if you want to blast your sour cream in her pink taco, in the back of a Chevy Tahoe- your arms better be FN swole!"

Fun fact- this was the very first Taco Tuesday video we filmed. In later Taco Tuesday videos I began to incorporate more Spanish phrases into the quotes.

"On Wednesday we do arms, cuz if you want to ram your beef where she makes a queef- your arms better be FN swole!"

"On Thursday we do arms, cuz if you want your trouser trout swimming in her clam cave, in the back of a Buick Enclave- your arms better be FN swole!"

"On Friday we do arms, cuz if you want a thick mami begging ya to eat her shitter, like a FN apple fritter- your arms better be FN swole!"

"On Saturday we do arms, cuz if you wanna be in the back of a Hummer, cleaning out her pipes like a motherfuckin plumber- your arms better be FN swole!"

"On Sunday we do arms, cuz if you want to blast your nut butter in her muff gutter, till she starts to fuckin stutter- your arms better be fu fu fu FN swole!"

Fun fact- we laughed for about 20 minutes non stop after this video. Zach almost passed out he was laughing so hard. This was one of the best performing videos we've ever done.

"On Monday we do chest, cuz if you want a thick mami giving you a Portuguese Snowblower, in the back of her Land Rover- your pecs better be FN swole!"

Fun fact- according to Urban Dictionary, a Portuguese Snowblower is when you have a girl naked on all fours and you line her asshole with cocaine. She then proceeds to fart, blowing the cocaine in your face. That is the Portuguese Snowblower. You're welcome...

"On Taco Tuesday we do arms, cuz if you want a thick mami screaming pon tus chorizo donde cago, in the back of an El Dorado- your arms better be FN swole!"

Fun fact- English translation is "put your sausage where I take a shit".

"On Wednesday we do arms, cuz if you want slap your beef hose on her nose till you dispose on her toes- your arms better be FN swole!"

"On Thursday we do arms, cuz if you want your bacon bazooka blasting goo on her labia, in a GMC Acadia- your arms better be FN swole!"

"On Friday we do arms, cuz if you want your pecker sauce running down her crack, in a Subaru Outback- your arms better be FN swole!"

Fun fact- this video was stitched by a popular TikTok chick who recreated this video implying that if a girl is in a Subaru Outback, she's most likely a lesbian and wouldn't want your pecker sauce running down her crack. The video went viral.

"On Saturday we do arms, cuz if you wanna slam those lips between her hips- your arms better be FN swole!"

"On Sunday we do arms, cuz if you want your nuts banging off her chin, at the Budget Inn- your arms better be FN swole!"

"On Monday we do chest, cuz if you want to blast your man milk all over her areola, in the back of a Corolla- your pecs better be FN swole!"

"On Taco Tuesday we do arms, cuz if you want a thick mami screaming pon tus palito de puerko in mi estomago, in the back of a Bronco- your arms better be FN swole!"

Fun fact- English translation is "put your little pork stick in my stomach". You're welcome.

"On Wednesday we do arms, cuz if you want a chick snacking on your sack, like Hunter Biden smoking crack- your arms better be FN swole!"

"On Thursday we do arms, cuz if you want to get thick chicks in a jiffy all over your stiffy- your arms better be FN swole!"

"On Friday we do arms, cuz if you want to stick your baloney pony in her meat pie, in the back of a Nissan Quashqui- your arms better be FN swole!"

"On Saturday we do arms, cuz if you want a thick mami named Maria taking your chorizo where she makes diarrhea- your arms better be FN swole!"

"On Sunday we do arms, cuz if you want a chick with a pretty face having your pecker paste running down her waist, your arms better be FN swole!"

"On Monday we do chest, cuz if you want a chick in leggings that are light gray, taking your beef bus up her Hershey Highway- your pecs better be FN swole!"

"On Tuesday we do arms, cuz if you want your ball bag tapping on her taint, till she starts to FN faint- your arms better be FN swole!"

Fun fact- in the video as I was saying "better be FN swole" I actually fainted and slid down the Hoist Bicep machine and fell to the floor. The video has well over 5M views in less than a week.

"On Wednesday we do arms, cuz if you want a chick with juicy buns, taking your beef where she has the runs- your arms better be FN swole!"

On Thursday we do arms, cuz if you want a thick mami beggin ya to leave something gooey dripping out of where she makes poopie- your arms better be FN swole!"

On Friday we do chest, cuz if you want to jam her clam, in a Dodge FN Ram- your pecs better be FN swole!"

Fun fact- this is the only Friday/Chest combination I've done in the 2+ years I've been doing these quotes. This video has a cameo by Mopar Brody one of my fellow Steel Supplements brothers.

"On Saturday we do arms, cuz if you want your pork stick stuffin her juicy musty muffin- your arms better be FN swole!"

"On Sunday we do arms, cuz if you wanna jam your love plunger up her shit cannon, in the back of her grandmas station wagon- your arms better be FN swole!"

"On Monday we do chest, cuz if you want to splash your groin gravy on the hot chick at Old Navy- your pecs better be FN swole!"

"On Taco Tuesday we do arms, cuz if you want a thick mami screamin dame tu leche de hombre en mi ojo, in the back of a Chevy Tahoe- your arms better be FN swole!"

Fun fact- English translation is "give me your man milk in my eye". This is also the second time I've reused a car name. Chevy Tahoe just rhymed perfectly!

"On Wednesday we do arms, cuz if you want to make a thick midget fidget, while you're motorboating her whisker biscuit- your arms better be FN swole!"

Fun fact- this video was pulled by TikTok for violating community guidelines. I guess I am not allowed to say midget?

"On Thursday we do arms, cuz if you wanna stick your one-eyed genie up in her pink panini- your arms better be FN swole!"

"On Friday we do arms, cuz if you want your lil soldier filling up her sausage holster- your arms better be FN swole!"

"On Saturday we do arms, cuz if you wanna slam your pork pistol up in her shit whistle- your arms better be FN swole!"

"On Sunday we do arms, cuz if you wanna slam your meat wrench all up in her stench trench- your arms better be FN swole!"

"On Monday we do chest, cuz if you want to give a thick granny the shocker, while she's sitting in her rocker- your pecs better be FN swole!"

"On Tuesday we do arms, cuz if you want to count the wrinkles on her stink star, in the back of a FN Jaguar- your arms better be FN swole!"

Fun fact- this video gained over 15M views in a little over a week all across social media. It's one of the more recent best performers! You can almost envision it!

"On Wednesday we do arms, cuz if you want a thick mami down on her knees, with her beef curtains flappin in the breeze- your arms better be FN swole!"

Fun fact- we were so fucking hungover when we filmed this video that we had to take a break after this one. Like I mentioned in the intro, we knock out at least 10 of these videos in a row back to back to back. Not after this one... we needed to take 5!

"On Thursday we do arms, cuz if you want a chick you met on the computer, taking your pork sword up her dookie shooter- your arms better be FN swole!"

"On Friday we do arms, cuz if you want your chowder cannon blasting goo in her fart box, in the back of a Chevy Equinox- your arms better be FN swole!"

"On Saturday we do arms, cuz if you want a chick with Monkey Pox tongue punching your fart box- your arms better be FN swole!"

Fun fact- this was the debut of Zach G in the background of the video. We filmed this in the gym at the Harrah's casino in Atlantic City NJ when the Monkey Pox hysteria was at its peak!

"On Sunday we do arms, cuz if you want a chick with a big rack massaging your ball sack- your arms better be FN swole!"

"On Monday we do chest, cuz if you want your moose knuckle rubbing up on her belt buckle- your pecs better be FN swole!"

"On Taco Tuesday we do arms, cuz if you want a thick mami screaming aye papi terminar en mi boca, and the back of a Range Rover- your arms better be FN swole!"

Fun fact- English translation is "oh daddy finish in my mouth!"

"On Wednesday we do arms, cuz if you want to take a chick out to dinner before you slam your meat in her shitter- your arms better be FN swole!"

"On Thursday we do arms, cuz if you want to give a chick an Alaskan Snow Dragon, in the back of a Volkswagen- your arms better be FN swole!"

Fun fact- according to Urban Dictionary, an Alaskan Snow Dragon is when you ejaculate in a chicks mouth and then punch her in the stomach so the jizz comes out her her nose. I don't condone punching anyone, but this shit is funny!

"On Friday we do arms, cuz if you want her beef flaps huggin your kielbasa, in the backseat of her Mazda- your arms better be FN swole!"

"On Saturday we do arms, cuz if you want Captain Winky in her brown eye that's all stinky- your arms better be FN swole!"

Fun fact- this video was also pulled by TikTok for violation community guidelines.

"On Sunday we do arms, cuz if you wanna spray your ball batter, all over her gallbladder- your arms better be FN swole!"

"On Monday we do chest, cuz if you want to give a chick a Cleveland Steamer, in the backseat of her Bimmer- your arms better be FN swole!"

Fun fact- according to urban dictionary, a Cleveland Steamer is taking a shit on someone's chest and then sitting on their chest and rolling back and forth smoothing out the shit. Disgusting if you ask me!

"On Tuesday we do arms, cuz if you want a thick mami droolin, while you're pushing her stool in- your arms better be FN swole!"

"On Wednesday we do arms, cuz if you want a chick going down on your meat pole in the back of a Kia Soul- your arms better be FN swole!"

Fun fact- when we filmed this video there were two smoking hot chicks on the machine next to us. Joey begged me not to say anything that was going to embarrass him. The rest is history. They ended up laughing and following me on IG.

"On Thursday we do arms, cuz if you're trying to shoot your ball snot, all over her G spot- your arms better be FN swole!"

"On Friday we do arms, cuz if you're trying to shove two in her pink and one in her stink, without buying her a drink- your arms better be FN swole!"

"On Saturday we do arms, cuz if you wanna be in a Ford Taurus blasting your baby gravy all over her clitoris- your arms better be FN swole!"

Fun fact- to make this rhyme I had to put extra emphasis on the word clit-or-US.

"On Sunday we do arms, cuz if you want to be like a wide receiver, going deep in her beaver- your arms better be FN swole!"

"On Monday we do chest, cuz if you want a chick flogging your dolphin, in the back of an Aston Martin- your pecs better be FN swole!"

Fun fact- according to Urban Dictionary, "flogging the dolphin" means to masturbate. Zach G said this term in passing and I knew I had to use it in a video!

"On Tuesday we do arms, cuz if you want to give a chick a pearl necklace, in the back of her Lexus- your arms better be FN swole!"

"On Wednesday we do arms, cuz if you want a chick drinking your pecker porridge, in the back of her Kia Sportage- your arms better be FN swole!"

"On Thursday we do arms, cuz if you want a thick mami down on her knees, taking your beef where she cuts the cheese- your arms better be FN swole!"

"On Friday we do arms, cuz if you wanna leave some meat stick leakage, all over her cleavage- your arms better be FN swole!"

"On Saturday we do arms, cuz if you want your pecker sauce running down her backside, in the back of a Kia Telluride- your arms better be FN swole!"

"On Sunday we do arms, cuz if you want to blast your man lube, in her fallopian tube- your arms better be FN swole!"

"On Monday we do chest, cuz if you want your pleasure pickle balls deep in her stink wrinkle- your pecs better be FN swole!"

"On Tuesday we do arms, cuz if you want to leave a cream pie in her balloon knot, in the back of her Fiat- your arms better be FN swole!"

"On Wednesday we do arms, cuz if you wanna stick your beef dart where she goes potty, in the back of your Maserati- your arms better be FN swole!"

"On Thursday we do arms, cuz if you want a thick mami draining your man mayo, in the back of an Alfa Romeo Stelvio- your arms better be FN swole!"

"On Friday we do arms, cuz if you wanna put a hurtin in the hole where she be squirtin- your arms better be FN swole!"

"On Saturday we do arms, cuz if you want a thick chick stroking your one eyed yogurt slinger, in the back of her Kia Stinger- your arms better be FN swole!"

"On Sunday we do arms, cuz if you wanna leave a cream pie in a Jehovah's Witness in the parking lot of Planet Fitness- your arms better be FN swole!"

Fun fact- this video was a Twitter exclusive. Although it's just a joke (but there are some hot Jehovah's Witness chicks) all the other platforms wouldn't understand the satire.

"On Monday we do chest, cuz if you wanna shove your pork rocket all up in her shit socket- your pecs better be FN swole!"

"On Taco Tuesday we do arms, cuz if you want a thick mami screaming pon tus los bolas en mi cabeza, in the back of an Impreza- your arms better be FN swole!"

Fun fact- English translation is "put your balls on my head".

"On Wednesday we do arms, cuz if you want her lips to pucker around your throbbing one eyed custard chucker- your arms better be FN swole!"

"On Thursday we do arms, cuz if you want a thick mami blowing on your skin flute, before you ram it up her poop chute- your arms better be FN swole!"

"On Friday we do arms, cuz if you're trying to pinch her nostrils, while your mushroom tip is tapping on her tonsils- your arms better be FN swole!"

"On Saturday we do arms, cuz if you want a thick chick going down on your one-eyed wonder weasel, in the back of a GMC diesel- your arms better be FN swole!"

"On Sunday we do arms, cuz if you want a chick named Margaret draining your beef hose in the back of a Target- your arms better be FN swole!"

"On Monday we do chest, cuz if you want to give a chick a Baltimore Brownie, in the back of her Audi- your pecs better be FN swole!"

Fun fact- according to Urban Dictionary, a "Baltimore Brownie" is when a guy takes a shit on a chick's head then proceeds to ejaculate on the shit. Who thinks of this shit?

"On Tuesday we do arms, cuz if you want the waitress at Outback making your T Bone erupt like volcanos, till you bust in the mashed potatoes- your arms better be FN swole!"

"On Wednesday we do arms, cuz if you want to put your cooter shooter in her pooper, in the back of her Mini Cooper- your arms better be FN swole!"

"On Thursdays we do arms, cuz if you want a chick drinking your cream of nut soup, in her 911 coupe- your arms better be FN swole!"

"On Friday we do arms, cuz if you want a chick squealin like a piggy, in the back of her Mercedes 550- your arms better be FN swole!"

"On Saturday we do arms, cuz if you want to splash her belly with your steamy creamy man jelly- your arms better be FN swole!"

"On Sunday we do arms, cuz if you want to shoot your juice where she drops a deuce- your arms better be FN swole!"

"In Pride Month we do legs, cuz if you're a broccoli head tucking your sweats in your socks wearing crocs, before you feast on some cocks- your legs better be FN swole!"

Fun fact- I do one leg day video a year for Pride Month. Men do legs for the adulation of other men, which is suspect. If I see a bro in the gym doing legs, I automatically assume he's gay.

"On Tuesday we do arms, cuz if you want to stick your pork noodle in her apple strudel, while she's out walking her poodle- your arms better be FN swole!"

"On Wednesday we do arms, cuz if you want a chick that's hotter than Venus, all over your penis- your arms better be FN swole!"

"On Thursday we do arms, cuz if you're trying to shove your stump where she takes a dump- your arms better be FN swole!"

"After surgery we do arms, cuz if you want a thick nurse pulling out your catheter, before you ram it up her shit blaster- your arms better be FN swole!"

Fun fact- I filmed this video as soon as I got out of surgery. The anesthesia pump hits different. I don't even remember filming it, but I am glad I did. It is the 3rd most viewed video on my TikTok page with 12M views! This video was filmed by my father, BobColts.

"On Saturday we do arms, cuz if you wanna be balls deep in her queef chamber, in the back of a Ford Ranger- your arms better be FN swole!"

"On Christmas Eve we do arms, cuz if you want a mistress with the thickness giving you syphilis for Christmas- your arms better be FN swole!"

Fun fact- Christmas Eve fell on a Sunday. This is another one where we laughed for a good 5 minutes after filming. Good times.

"On Monday we do chest, cuz if you wanna slam your beef in her shit dispenser, in the back of a Dodge Avenger- your pecs better be FN swole!"

"On Tuesday we do arms, cuz if you wanna make her lipstick smudge, while you're clappin them cheeks packing her fudge- your arms better be FN swole!"

"On Thursday we do arms, cuz if you're trying to stab her with your pork needle, in the back of a Volkswagen Beetle- your arms better be FN swole!"

"On Friday we do arms, cuz if you want to give a chick an Anaheim Knuckle Buster, in the back of a Plymouth Duster- your arms better be FN swole!"

Fun fact- according to Urban Dictionary, an "Anaheim Knuckle Buster" is when you ejaculate on your fist and then punch someone in the face. Again, I do not condone punching anyone. This is satire and the term is fucking hysterical!

"On Saturday we do arms, cuz if you want a thick chick munchin on your cheese fromunda, in the back of a Toyota Tundra- your arms better be FN swole!"

"On Sunday we do arms, cuz if you're trying to shove your cock in her meat sock, while she's scrolling on TikTok- your arms better be FN swole!"

"On Monday we do chest, cuz if you're trying to dunk your little fella, all up in her fecal cellar- your pecs better be FN swole!"

"On Tuesday we do arms, cuz if you want to put your trouser snake in her beaver hole, in the back of a Del Sol- your arms better be FN swole!"

"On Wednesday we do arms, cuz if you want a thick Guatemalan all over your Johnson- your arms better be FN swole!"

"On Thursday we do arms, cuz if you want a chick with glutes like a fruit to blow on your flute- your arms better be FN swole!"

"On Friday we do arms, cuz if you want to paint her guts with your man jam, in the back of a Trans Am- your arms better be FN swole!"

Fun fact- Yes, I am aware that Trans Am's do not have back seats.

"On Saturday we do arms, cuz if you want to make a thick chick quiver, while your ball sauce is squirting on her liver- your arms better be FN swole!"

"On Sunday we do arms, cuz if you want a chick choking on your boner in the back of a Tacoma- your arms better be FN swole!"

Fun fact- the emphasis needs to be on the Tac-om-uh to rhyme with bone-uh. You're welcome.

"On Monday we do chest, cuz if you want a thick chick slobbin on your knob, like corn on the cob- your pecs better be FN swole!"

"On Taco Tuesday we do arms, cuz if you want a thick mami screamin aye papi don't stoppy, in the back of your jalopy- your arms better be FN swole!"

Fun fact- English translation is "oh daddy don't stop" and a "jalopy" is just an old beat up car/truck.

"On Wednesday we do arms, cuz if you want a thick mami feelin on your guns, before she gives up the buns- your arms better be FN swole!"

"On Thursday we do arms, cuz if you wanna spray your salty nut soup where she takes a poop- your arms better be FN swole!"

"On Friday we do arms, cuz if you wanna drill her with your pecker, like a Black & FN Decker- your arms better be FN swole!"

"On Saturday we do arms, cuz if you want a chick beggin you to hump her, right in her dumper- your arms better be FN swole!"

"On Sunday we do arms, cuz if you want a chick with thick thighs taking your money shot right between her eyes- your arms better be FN swole!"

"On Monday we do chest, cuz if you want to shoot your man goo on the hot chick at the barbeque- your pecs better be FN swole!"

"On Taco Tuesday we do arms, cuz if you want a thick mami screaming dame tu leche de hombre en mi ojo, in the back of a Chevy Tahoe- your arms better be FN swole!"

Fun fact- English translation is "give me your man milk in my eye". Weird request, but whatever.

"On Wednesday we do arms, cuz if you want your baby gravy shooting out of your weenie, all over her bikini- your arms better be FN swole!"

"On Thursday we do arms, cuz if you want a chick begging you to go harder, in the back of a Dodge Charger- your arms better be FN swole!"

"On Friday we do arms, cuz if you wanna jam your pork pumper all up in her shit dumper- your arms better be FN swole!"

"On Saturday we do arms, cuz if you want your ball snot splashing her balloon knot- your arms better be FN swole!"

"On Sunday we do arms, cuz if you want to blast your creamy mash all up in her juicy gash- your arms better be FN swole!"

"On Monday we do chest, cuz if you want a thick chick going down on your piss stick- your pecs better be FN swole!"

"On Tuesday we do arms, cuz if you want to stick your zipper twix where she shits out chocolate bricks- your arms better be FN swole!"

"On Wednesday we do arms, cuz if you want to drown her with your pecker ooze in the back of a Chevy Cruze- your arms better be FN swole!"

"On Thursday we do arms, cuz if wanna give a chick a greasy pierre, till you bust in her hair- your arms better be FN swole!"

Fun fact- according to Urban Dictionary, a "Greasy Pierre" is when you rub your penis up and down a woman's ass crack. You're welcome.

"On Friday we do arms, cuz if you're trying to get a handy from a stripper named Candy, in the back of her Camry- your arms better be FN swole!"

"On Saturday we do arms, cuz if you want a thick mami to slobber on your blue veined throbber- your arms better be FN swole!"

"On Sunday we do arms, cuz if you want to give a chick a Wisconsin Blow Dryer, while listening to the Foo Fighters- your arms better be FN swole!"

Fun fact- according to Urban Dictionary, a "Wisconsin Blow Dryer" is the art of ejaculating on a chicks face, then farting in her face to dry the jizz. You're welcome.

"On Monday we do chest, cuz if you want a chick pecking on your pecker like a parrot, while shes waxing your carrot- your pecs better be FN swole!"

"On Halloween we do arms, cuz if you want a thick mummy taking your ball sauce all over their tummy- your arms better be FN swole!"

"On Wednesday we do arms, cuz if you want to count the creases in her stink ring, in the back of a Sebring- your arms better be FN swole!"

"On Thanksgiving we do arms, cuz if you want a thick chick whipping your little pilgrim outta your trousers, in the back of the Mayflower- your arms better be FN swole!"

Fun fact- I posted this video this Thanksgiving. I wasn't in love with the quote because it really doesn't rhyme, and you can visibly see how annoyed I was as soon as I say "mayflowers" in the video. Go back and watch! Thanksgiving 2023!

"On Friday we do arms, cuz if you want to take a thick chick to the movies and bust a nut on her boobies- your arms better be FN swole!"

"On St. Patrick's Day we do arms, cuz if you want a chick skipping the corned beef and cabbage to go down on your package- your arms better be FN swole!"

"On Sunday we do arms, cuz if you want to stick your wee wee where she makes pee pee- your arms better be FN swole!"

Fun fact- as childish as this rhyme is, I couldn't post it on the main social media platforms because it would get flagged instantly. I posted it as a Twitter/X exclusive and people loved it!

"On Monday we do chest, cuz if you want a chick you met on Skype, taking your pork sword up her fart pipe- your arms better be FN swole!"

"On Taco Tuesday we do arms, cuz if you want a thick mami screaming dame crème en mi garganta, in the back of an Elantra- your arms better be FN swole!"

Fun fact- English translation is "give me cream in my throat".

"On Wednesday we do arms, cuz if you wanna pop her in her turd chopper, then go on Instagram and block her- your arms better be FN swole!"

"On Thursday we do arms, cuz if you want a thick chick stroking your purple headed pelvis poker, in the backseat of her Land Rover- your arms better be FN swole!"

"On Friday we do arms, cuz if you want a chick with glutes like a pumpkin giving you a blumpkin- your arms better be FN swole!"

Fun fact- according to Urban Dictionary, a "Blumpkin" is the act of getting a blowjob while taking a shit. This was also the first video that I broke character and couldn't keep a straight face. I mean how could I? Blumpkin is a funny FN word!

"On Saturday we do arms, cuz if you want a thick chick with daddy issues, draining your pecker till you run out of tissues- your arms better be FN swole!"

"On Sunday we do arms, cuz if you want a thick chick down on her knees, whipping your zipper sausage outta your dungarees- your arms better be FN swole!"

"On Monday we do chest, cuz if you want a chick blowing on your ham candle, till your weiner wax drips on her sandal- your pecs better be FN swole!"

"On Tuesday we do arms, cuz if you want a thick mami making your knob throb, while she gives you a rim job- your arms better be FN swole!"

"On Wednesday we do arms, cuz if you want a chick spanking your monkey, till she gets something chunky- your arms better be FN swole!"

"On Thursday we do arms, cuz if you want a chick that's all tatted tossing your salad- your arms better be FN swole!"

"On Friday we do arms, cuz if you want to clap more cheeks than Will Smith at the Oscar's, before you blast off on her knockers- your arms better be FN swole!"

Fun fact- this video was filmed around the time Will Smith slapped Chris Rock at the Oscar's.

"On Saturday we do arms, cuz if you wanna shoot your meat sauce all over her lip gloss- your arms better be FN swole!"

Fun fact- this was my first TikTok video to break 5M views!

"On Sunday we do arms, cuz if you want a thick chick leaving rings of lipstick around your meat stick- your arms better be FN swole!"

"On Monday we do chest, cuz if you want to blast your goo where she takes a poo, in the Chick-Fil-A drive-thru- your pecs better be FN swole!"

"On Tuesday we do arms, cuz if you want a thick chick losing control, while your meat pole is up in her bunghole- your arms better be FN swole!"

"On Wednesday we do arms, cuz if you want a thick mami down on her knees, spraying your ball cheese with a can of Frebeze- your arms better be FN swole!"

"On Thursday we do arms, cuz if you wanna dump your semen sauce in her crap cavern, in the back of a Saturn- your arms better be FN swole!"

"On Friday we do arms, cuz if you want her stinky brown eye winkin, in the back of a Lincoln- your arms better be FN swole!"

"On Saturday we do arms, cuz if you're tryna find her vagina, in the back of a Pathfinder- your arms better be FN swole!"

Fun fact- you have to put the emphasis on "FINDA" instead of find her and "PATHFINDA" instead of Pathfinder to make this rhyme. Sometimes you have to get creative with it!

"On Sunday we do arms, cuz if you want to stick your scrotum totem in her crapper, in the back of a Ford Raptor- your arms better be FN swole!"

Outro

I'm sure by this point you are either super motivated to go fuck up the weights or your stomach hurts from laughing your ass off. Or both. I would like to take this time to introduce you to the people who make these quotes come to life in video form all over social media:

Joey Bags: Joey was the first person to start filming these quotes for me when I got out of the hospital. It was his idea to start the videos pointing at my sneakers and then slowly panning up to my face before I started speaking. He would beg me not to be loud or make a scene while doing these, so obviously I did the opposite and embarrassed the shit out of him. Joey is responsible for filming probably 50 of these quotes and they would not exist without his help!

Alex: I met Alex when I first got my colostomy bag removed and got the green light to go back to lifting in March 2022. He was a salesman/front desk employee at the gym and recognized me as soon as I walked in. One day Joey wasn't available and there was a quote/video that I needed to film, and I asked Alex if he would help me out and the rest is history. There would be times that Alex would drop whatever he was doing to go out of his way to meet me at the gym to film a video or two. Not only is Alex the ONLY person I fully trust to film these quotes, but he's also now a cohost on the Glorious House of GAINZ Podcast and one of my best friends. The Latin Heartthrob is the FN man!

Zach G: If you're ever wondering who is choking in the background of the more recent videos, that would be Zach. I met Zach through social media back in 2017 and over recent years he's become part of my inner circle and a cohost on the Glorious House of GAINZ podcast. It would feel weird doing these videos/quotes without having Zach in the background. His laugh is contagious, and he adds a lot to the presentation. Fun fact, Zach also drives 6hrs from Pittsburgh to meet us in Atlantic City NJ every few weeks just to get these videos done.

There have also been a handful of people who have filmed a video or two for me that I wanted to mention. Bobcolts (my father), Ray Vegaz, VinCenz0, Nick Smith, and Fresko Fadez. If I forgot a name or two it's because you aren't that important, or the video sucked.

SPECIAL THANKS

I would like to thank my parents for making me.

Marissa for putting up with me and taking care of me when I was dying.

Jason Huh and Steel Supplements for employing me and allowing me to quit my 9-5 to play a meathead on social media for a living.

Omni Energy Drink for keeping me caffeinated.

Ray Vegaz, VinCenzo, Joey Bags, POTY, BeardSoStrong, Jimmy Triceps, MBJ, Kayleigh, The Latin Heartthrob Alex, Megan, and Zach G for keeping me company on the Glorious House of Gainz Podcast every week since 2018.

Rockstar Booty Mike Marinaccio for allowing me to film inappropriate videos at the MEGA Fairfield Retro Fitness.

Paul Huh for filming me in 4K and creating this bad ass book cover.

Low Fat Pat and Bethany for being the best security team a bro could ask for.

Megan "The Harami Mami" and Jas for helping us film behind-the-scenes content of our Better Be FN Swole, and Gym Etiquette videos.

12 Gauge and Angry Will for helping me become a SoundCloud rapper.

Alex from TopLine SMP, Lou from Maestro's, and Fresko from Fresko Fadez for keeping me fresh.

My Patreon family for being the real MVPs.

Amiri King for talking me off the social media ledge over and over again.

And finally, Robert Keoseyan for holding my hand through this book writing process.

If I forgot anyone, don't take it personal. My memory is shot.

EPILOGUE
EVOLUTION OF THE VIDEOS

With everything in life, once you do something over and over again for a while it begins to get stale. I have a really good sense of when things are starting to run their course and it's time to switch shit up. Obviously, not everyone is going to like changes being made to things they like, and you get your handful of haters online who make their grievances known.

I'll give you an example- with my Car Rage videos from 2016-2020, go back to the first 10 Car Rage videos and then go watch the last 10 Car Rage videos. Same presentation, but totally different. In the beginning the Car Rage videos were just me screaming about whatever I was mad at that week. Then over time I incorporated some rhyming words within the videos and little catch phrases that viewers would comment back to me in the comment section.

Same thing happened with the Better Be FN Swole videos. At first, I used my normal voice to say some of the most boring lines known to man. "On Monday we do chest, because swollen pecs leads to sex". No inflection and no growl.

Just plain old Rob spitting lines and Joey filming. Now I've made the growl a staple. Every video has inflection and I sound like I chew on gravel before I execute my lines. The code words I use are to trick the algorithm. I've been muted and had more than my fair share of posts removed for violating guidelines. Trust me, I would much rather say "dick" and "pussy", but I have to replace them with "pork sword" and "sausage holster". I guess in a way, it makes them funnier.

In the beginning, Joey and I would film one video per night. If I needed a video for a Monday night to post at 10pm, we would film the video around 9pm and I would edit/subtitle while I was on the treadmill, and it would go up on social media that night.

When Alex took over the reigns of being my full time cameraman, we pretty much followed the same template. Sometimes we would film two or three just incase he wasn't working at the gym for a few days. At least I had content in the bank.

Now that I live in Florida, this all changed. I've been flying up to New Jersey every 6-8 weeks just so I can Alex film and have Zach in the background. We are the dream team. Can I get someone here in Florida to film these for me? Sure, I can- but it wouldn't be the same. Alex's ability to hold the camera steady as he's laughing his ass off is a talent in itself. Zach sounding like he smokes 8 packs a day (which he does not) choking in the background adds the secret sauce we never knew we needed.

So the new formula is complicated, but we make it work. Zach drives 6hrs from Pittsburgh PA and meets us in Atlantic City NJ. I fly in from Sarasota Florida and meet Zach in Atlantic City. We then head 2hrs to central NJ and meet Alex at Crunch Fitness. We drink about half a bottle of Jack Daniels in the parking lot, catch up for a few minutes, then go in and knock 10-15 of these out in a row. I've mentioned this in the introduction, but just a reminder that Alex and Zach are hearing the quotes for the very first time, so their reaction is genuine and organic AF. Mix in the alcohol and the fact we're all a bunch of simpletons that we find words like "goo" and "poo" fucking hilarious. Once we have 10-15 good ones in the drafts, Zach and I head back to Atlantic City and Alex goes his own way and we meet up later that night to celebrate with the rest of the crew

I know this section is a little "inside baseball" for a lot of you and you don't give a shit about the fine details. However, there is a good chunk of people who love the behind-the-scenes stuff. Now that all the secrets are revealed, at least you know why we are laughing so hard and having a fucking blast! Based on the comment section, I know most of you are right there with us, and we appreciate you!

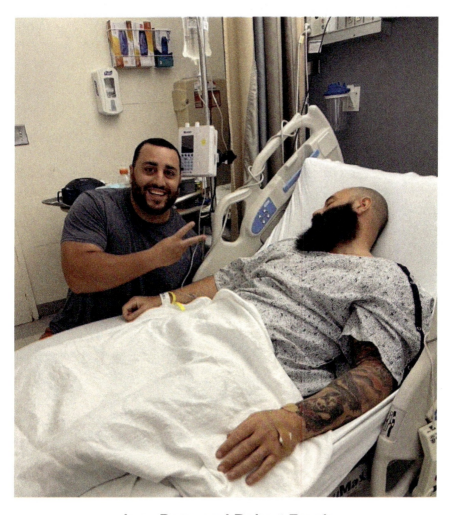
Joey Bags and Robert Frank

Left to right, Ray Vegaz, Megan, Robert Frank, Alex, Jas, and Zach G

FOLLOW ME ON SOCIAL MEDIA:

Instagram- @robertfrank615 , @robert_frank615 , @robertfrankreels , @gloriouspodcast

Facebook- @robertfrank615

YouTube- @robertfrank615

TikTok- @robertfrank615, @robert_frank615

Twitter/X - @robertfrank615

Patreon- @robertfrank615

Podcast- Glorious House of Gainz Podcast (new episodes available on Patreon.com/robertfrank615)

Robertfrank615 Merchandise (tee shirts & more) – Robertfrank615.com

Steel Supplements/Omni Energy Drink - Steelsupps615.com

Personalized Videos- Cameo.com/robertfrank615

Printed in Great Britain
by Amazon